The Lion Who
Wanted to Love

Also written by Giles Andreae
and illustrated by David Wojtowycz

Rumble in the Jungle

A noisy collection
of animal poems

ORCHARD BOOKS
96 Leonard Street, London EC2A 4RH
Orchard Books Australia
14 Mars Road, Lane Cove, NSW 2066
1 86039 441 8
First Published in Great Britain in 1997
Text copyright © Purple Enterprises Ltd. 1997
Illustrations copyright © David Wojtowycz 1997
The right of Giles Andreae to be identified as the author and David Wojtowycz
as the illustrator of this work has been asserted by them in accordance with the
Copyright, Designs and Patents Act, 1988.
A CIP catalogue for this book is available from the British Library.
Printed in Belgium

The Lion Who Wanted to Love

Giles Andreae

David Wojtowycz

✸ ORCHARD BOOKS ✸

To Victoria
G.A

For T.C and T.D
D.W.

Deep in the African heartland
Way out on the hot sunny plains,
There lived a small lion who didn't fit in
And Leo was this lion's name.

Now lions are usually fierce
And lions are meant to be strong,
But Leo just wanted to love everybody
And play with his friends all day long.

"You worry me, Leo, my darling,"
His mum started saying one day.
"You'll never survive in the animal world
If you don't learn to hunt for your prey."

"But, Mummy," said Leo, bewildered,
"I don't think I quite understand.
I'm sure there are plenty of lions that hunt
Who could kill all the beasts in the land."

"And besides, when I'm close to a zebra
A funny thought goes through my head,
Instead of deciding to bite through his skin
I'd much rather hug him instead."

"I have spoken," said Leo's mum sternly.
"It's up to you now to decide,
But if you insist you're not going to hunt,
Then there's no place for you in our pride."

Poor Leo crept off to the jungle
But hoped that with love in his heart,
He'd learn how to cope in the animal world
Though he didn't quite know where to start.

That evening while Leo was sleeping
He woke to the thunder of hooves,
And when he looked up from his lair he could see
A whole antelope herd on the move.

Some leopards were running beside them
Surrounded by thick clouds of dust,
Leo thought quickly, he jumped to his feet,
"I must help them!" he cried. "Yes, I must!"

Then he caught sight of two injured young ones
Who couldn't keep up with the bunch,
If he didn't help them to try to escape
The leopards would eat them… for lunch!

Leo led them away back to safety
And gave them some food they could eat.
He licked their wounds clean till they both became strong
And he nursed them back onto their feet.

The antelope babies kissed Leo
And told him, "We'll never forget
That you saved our lives when we thought we were dead,
You're the loveliest lion we've met."

Leo was very excited
His face had lit up in a smile
"It's fun making friends in the jungle," he thought.
Then he lay down and slept for a while.

From that day on Leo decided
To run to each squeal and each cry.
He led little hippos to watering holes
And he taught baby birds how to fly.

He helped a giraffe who'd been injured
And a vulture who'd broken his wing,
And even though all of his friends gave him food,
He never once asked for a thing.

Then one day beside a wide river
Leo heard a small animal scream,
He ran to the banks and caught sight of a cheetah
Being swept very quickly downstream.

"Please help!" cried the cheetah in panic,
"I haven't yet learned how to swim,
The waterfall's going to drown me, I'm sure!"
With a splash, Leo boldly leapt in.

He managed to rescue the cheetah
And push him quite safe to the side,
But as he was trying to scramble ashore
Leo slipped and got caught in the tide.

The river was crashing and foaming
And Leo let out a loud yelp,
The waterfall wasn't too far away now,
So the cheetah rushed off to find help.

The friends Leo had in the jungle
All raced to the bank straight away

They wanted so much to show Leo their thanks
At last they had now found a way.

They climbed on the rocks through the rapids
And linked themselves up tail and paw.
An elephant wrapped his long trunk round a tree
Which anchored them safe to the shore.

And when Leo got to the rapids
A lioness dipped down her head.
She lifted him gently across to the bank,
"You're safe, Leo darling," she said.

"My son, you're a brave little lion,"
She spoke in her humblest tone.
"I was wrong, now I see love can bring us together,
Please, Leo," she said, "come back home."

"You've got to be strong to be different,
And when you've got love on your side
You've got the most valuable gift that there is,
We want you as King of our pride."